T0401436

MORE THAN MEETS THE EYE

ADHD

WRITTEN BY
Kirsty Holmes

KidHaven
PUBLISHING

Published in 2025 by
KidHaven Publishing, an Imprint of
Greenhaven Publishing, LLC
2544 Clinton St., Buffalo, NY 14224

© 2024 BookLife Publishing Ltd.

Written by: Kirsty Holmes
Edited by: Rebecca Phillips-Bartlett
Designed by: Ker Ker Lee

Cataloging-in-Publication Data

Names: Holmes, Kirsty.
Title: ADHD / Kirsty Holmes.
Description: Buffalo, New York : KidHaven
    Publishing, 2025. | Series: More than meets
    the eye | Includes glossary and index.
Identifiers: ISBN 9781534547582 (pbk.) |
    ISBN 9781534547599 (library bound) |
    ISBN 9781534547605 (ebook)
Subjects: LCSH: Attention-deficit hyperactivity
    disorder--Juvenile literature.
Classification: LCC RJ506.H9 H656 2025 |
    DDC 618.92'8589--dc23

Manufactured in the United States of America

CPSIA compliance information: Batch #CSKH25
For further information contact Greenhaven Publishing LLC at 1-844-317-7404.

Please visit our website, www.greenhavenpublishing.com.
For a free color catalog of all our high-quality books, call toll free 1-844-317-7404.

Find us on

ABOUT THIS BOOK

"ADHD is not about knowing what to do, but about doing what one knows."
(Dr. Russell Barkley)

This book was written by an author with ADHD, for children with ADHD and their allies.

GLOSSARY WORDS

As you read, you will see some words that look like **this**. The meaning of these words can be found in the glossary on page 31.

CONTENTS

KEY VOCABULARY

Whether you have ADHD yourself, are an **ally** to the ADHD community, or you're here to find out about ADHD, there are some important words you will need to know as you read this book.

NEURODIVERGENT AND NEUROTYPICAL

Neurodivergence and neurotypicality are neurotypes — different types of human brain. Most people in the world (around 80%) are neurotypical. This means their brains are seen as the "typical" human brain.

Around 15% to 20% of the world's population is thought to be neurodivergent. A neurodivergence is a brain difference where the brain works differently than a neurotypical person's brain. There are lots of types of neurodivergence. This means that people with different types of brains will have different strengths and face different challenges.

An example of a neurodivergence is ADHD. Another example is autism spectrum disorder.

> I have ADHD. I am neurodivergent.

> I am dyslexic, so I am also neurodivergent.

These other conditions are also recognized as neurodivergences:

- Developmental speech disorders
- Dyslexia
- Dysgraphia
- Dyspraxia
- Dyscalculia
- Dysnomia
- Intellectual **disability**
- Tourette's syndrome

Neurodiversity is a word that describes all of the different neurotypes together. A group that includes people with different neurotypes is a neurodiverse group. Humanity is neurodiverse.

DYSPRAXIAL

ADHD

NEUROTYPICAL

DYSLEXIA

AUTISTIC

IDENTITY FIRST OR PERSON FIRST?

QUESTION: Should I say "ADHD person" or "person with ADHD"?

EXPLANATION:

Person-First Language: "I have ADHD" or "I am a person with ADHD"

This way of describing people with the ADHD neurotype puts their importance as a human first, and their difference or disability second. Many people think this is the more respectful choice, and some people think it is better to separate the person from their disability or difference this way. We have chosen to use this in this book.

But not everyone agrees — and not everyone has to use the same words to describe themselves.

Identity-First Language: "ADHD person" or "ADHD-er"

Some people prefer to recognize their condition or neurotype as an important part of who they are first. Putting "ADHD" before "person" reminds you that their neurotype is an important part of who they are, and not something they "have" separate from themselves.

ANSWER: If you have ADHD, you can choose which language you prefer. If you are talking to or about a person with ADHD, it's polite to ask them which they prefer.

WHAT IS ADHD?

A TERRIBLE NAME FOR A BRILLIANT BRAIN

Unfortunately, ADHD was named a while ago, and we didn't know as much about it then as we do now.

ATTENTION DEFICIT

WHICH MEANS:
Can't focus on anything

HYPERACTIVITY

WHICH MEANS:
Can't sit still, always moving, fidgety in the body

DISORDER

WHICH MEANS:
A disease or problem

Now, we know a lot more about ADHD, so we know this is a terrible name!

We know now that people with ADHD can focus, sometimes much more than anyone around us — but we can't control where that focus goes. We know that being hyperactive can mean a very busy body OR a very busy brain — or both! We know that not everyone with ADHD will be hyperactive at all. And we know that ADHD isn't a disease, or anything "wrong" with us: ADHD is just a normal (if different) way of being human.

Four times three... Oh! A butterfly!

... and four times three is...? James? Are you listening?

People with ADHD are born this way and will have ADHD all their lives. The ADHD brain is just built the way it is.

6

ATTENTION

ADHD doesn't mean we can't pay attention — we just have trouble focusing our attention on one thing at a time. We are easily distracted because we want to pay attention to everything all the time! It's not a lack of attention — it's a lack of control.

We can find it hard to target our attention. Or we might get so focused on something that we forget everything else (hyperfocus).

HYPERACTIVITY

Hyperactivity means being active all the time, or much more than most people. Someone who is hyperactive will feel driven to move, as if they have a motor making them go, go, go! Hyperactive people find it very difficult to stop, sit still, or be at rest.

Hyperactivity in the body can come out as fidgeting, **stimming**, or finding it impossible to sit still.

Is Claire mad at me?

My sneakers are tight.

Did I say the right thing?

Can dogs hear music?

Did I do my math homework?

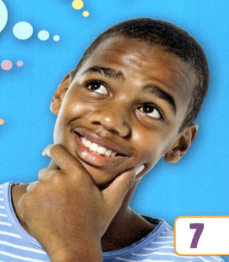

Hyperactivity can also be in the mind. This can feel like having lots of thoughts at once or having "too much" going on in the brain. A racing mind can keep you from falling asleep, but also means you are a big thinker with lots of ideas.

Hyperactivity can be a big part of ADHD, or a person with ADHD might not be hyperactive at all.

TRAITS OF ADHD

ADHD is a condition made of a range of traits, strengths, and challenges.

ATTENTION AND FOCUS

- Is good at multitasking
- Can't concentrate for long
- Is able to hyperfocus
- Is easily distracted
- Notices every little detail and spots things others miss
- Daydreams
- Makes little mistakes all the time
- Forgets things, such as lunch or the time
- Is easily bored
- Struggles to listen
- Has trouble remembering instructions

HYPERACTIVITY AND IMPULSIVENESS

- Can't sit still/fidgets
- Talks a lot, is a "chatterbox"
- Has difficulty taking turns
- Has big ideas
- Struggles to wait
- Has endless energy
- Jumps in without thinking
- Has a big imagination
- Interrupts others
- Is enthusiastic
- Does risky things
- Is brave
- Shouts out in class
- Thinks creatively
- Is good at problem solving
- Has lots of energy and excitement
- Loves trying new things

EMOTIONS

- Has big feelings
- Has difficulty controlling feelings
- Has a strong sense of right and wrong
- Struggles to know what we are feeling
- Has **empathy** for others

EXECUTIVE FUNCTION

- Has trouble with understanding time
- Forgets to do life skills such as eating
- Is disorganized
- Has trouble getting tasks started

Not everyone with ADHD will have all of these traits. Some traits cause us problems and some help us out.

TYPES OF ADHD

ADHD can be divided into three main types:

Inattentive Type

- Most traits have to do with attention: focus, listening, and remembering

- Easily distracted, a "daydreamer"

- Trouble keeping attention on one thing at a time

- More girls are **diagnosed** with this type of ADHD

Hyperactive-Impulsive Type

- Most traits have to do with hyperactivity or impulsivity: interrupting, acting without thinking

- Always moving, a "chatterbox" or "fidgety"

- Impatient, interrupts and speaks without thinking

- More boys are diagnosed with this type of ADHD

Combined Type

- Split between attentive, hyperactive, and impulsive traits

- Most people with ADHD have this type, both boys and girls

ADHD symptoms can change over time, so the type of ADHD you have can change too.

"EVERYONE'S A LITTLE BIT ADHD, RIGHT?"

Most traits of ADHD are just regular human things that everyone does. Everyone forgets sometimes or gets distracted. But this doesn't mean everyone has "a little bit of" ADHD. People with ADHD experience these things all the time. Most people don't forget their lunch every day or get distracted all the time. ADHD is a different way of being human, which is why neurotypical people relate to our traits. But the amount this happens and the difficulty we face because of these traits is what means that we have ADHD.

EXECUTIVE FUNCTION

GETTING THINGS DONE

We all use executive function (EF) skills as we go about our lives. Executive function skills help us learn, work, and look after ourselves. Your executive function is like the boss of your brain, helping you plan tasks and remember how to carry them out. We need these skills to listen, organize ourselves, start and finish jobs, and keep track of what we are doing and when.

MAKE A SANDWICH

CLEAN MY ROOM

DO HOMEWORK

BRUSH TEETH

DO CHORES

Many people with ADHD have trouble with EF skills. The bosses of our brains are not very good at getting the different parts to do their jobs properly or work together. Even if we know how to do something, such as make a sandwich or take a bath, actually being able to put all the skills together and get it done is another matter. This is why we can really want to do a task but find it difficult to actually do it.

Get up... Come on, get up...

We can get stuck trying to start something for hours, sometimes. No matter how much we want to do something, we just can't make ourselves do it. This is known as "task paralysis" or "freeze mode."

PRACTICE MAKES PROGRESS

Executive function skills can be learned, and with practice and the right support, many people with ADHD can manage their lives well.

Top Tips for Helping EF Skills:

- Write things down.

- Use a watch or timers.

- Give yourself a little reward for completing a task.

- Get enough sleep and rest and eat **high-protein meals**.

- Take lots of breaks! This will help you focus better in between.

- Be positive — give yourself lots of chances, restarts, and kind words.

- Move! Exercise (even a walk or a bit of dancing) helps the brain to function.

- Use bright calendars, picture planners, or colorful sticky notes.

- Keep it fun — the more you can turn a chore into a game, the more you will want to do it!

- A little bit of sugar can boost your brain's function. Try a few sips of lemonade before an exam or a chore.

- Do things with other people and ask for help when you need it.

If your planners look cool, you are more likely to use them. Get creative!

Technology, such as watches and phones, can store information so you don't have to remember it. They can remind you of things and help to keep you on time.

11

DOPAMINE

WHAT IS DOPAMINE?

Different parts of the brain are responsible for different jobs, such as memory, skills, or language. Brains use **chemicals** (called neurotransmitters) to carry messages between different parts of the brain and through the body. This is how the brain tells the body what to do — to breathe, sleep, have emotions, concentrate, or move.

One of the most important neurotransmitters for ADHD is called dopamine. If you have ADHD, you are going to hear a LOT about dopamine. Dopamine controls learning (knowing how to do stuff) and motivation (being able to get up and actually do it). It also helps us **regulate** pain, emotions, and feeling good when we have done something well.

This is what a **molecule** of dopamine looks like.

ADHD brains have a dopamine problem. We do make dopamine, but we don't seem to have as much, or we don't use it as well as neurotypical brains do. Think about the traits of ADHD — difficulty focusing, staying motivated, or getting up to do a seemingly simple job. All of these things are controlled by dopamine, so it's no wonder we struggle without it.

Dopamine hits ADHD brains hard and fast, so we can be REALLY motivated, but only for a short amount of time. This means we can be great in the moment, but struggle with long projects that take effort.

BOOST YOUR DOPAMINE

GET MOVING

Find a way to get moving — run, bounce, climb, dance, or play your favorite sport. During exercise, your body makes more dopamine, which helps regulate ADHD brains. Exercise also helps hyperactive people use their energy and feel less fidgety and more comfortable.

Complicated solo sports are best for ADHD, including martial arts, dance, ice-skating, gymnastics, climbing, and skateboarding. These tricky skills keep your brain really busy and focused — which would you like to try?

EAT RIGHT FOR YOUR NEUROTYPE

Eating these foods can boost dopamine, help with concentration, and look after the ADHD brain.

- Protein — lean meat, beans, fish, tofu, milk, eggs, cheese, lentils, and seeds
- Tyrosine — found in protein-rich foods, this helps the body make dopamine
- Omega 3 and 6 oils — these are oils found in fish such as salmon and tuna, soybeans, walnuts, pumpkin seeds, and eggs
- <u>Vitamins and minerals</u>, especially vitamin C, vitamin B6, iron, and zinc

MEDICATION

If you, your grown-ups, and your doctor think they will help you, medicines can help with the trickier traits of ADHD. Just like glasses help eyes to focus, ADHD medications help brains to focus better and ignore distractions.

MEMORY

ADHD AND MEMORY

There are three types of memory affected by ADHD: short-term, long-term, and working memory.

Long-term memories are big, important memories that your brain needs to store, like a library of all your life experiences, skills, and knowledge.

Short-term memories are small bits of information you only need for a short time, like a note on a scrap of paper.

People with ADHD can have problems with both long-term and short-term memory.

WORKING MEMORY

Working memory holds onto your short-term memories a little longer so you can use them. Think of this like the glue on a sticky note — the information will stick a little longer, but not forever. Working memory then uses long-term memory to turn the short-term instructions into an action. For example, if a teacher asks you "what is 2+2?", your short-term memory jots down the question, and your working memory holds it in place while it gets the answer from your long-term memory.

In the ADHD brain, the glue on our sticky notes just isn't as sticky. This means our short-term memories can easily get lost, and we can find it hard to follow instructions, plan tasks, or work with information, such as lists or numbers. We might have the answer in our long-term memory, but our working memory cannot connect the two things easily. This can make things at school or work tricky for people with ADHD, because there are lots of instructions to follow and tasks to complete, but our working memory can't keep up.

IMPROVE YOUR WORKING MEMORY

- Break tasks into small steps using checklists.
- Carry a little notebook and a pencil and get in the habit of writing everything into it — instructions, directions, anything you might forget (which is probably a lot!).
- Use pictures, glitter, and colors — fun helps your brain remember!
- Play memory games — try tongue twisters or hide-and-find games to improve your memory.
- Use the senses — put important information to music, trace letters with your fingers, or read aloud.
- Practice makes progress! Working memory gets stronger when you repeat things a lot.
- Use objects, stationery, and technology to help you.
  - Put reminders on sticky notes in places where you can't miss seeing them, and use them to remind you of the things you need.
  - Phones and tablets have apps, timers, sounds, and visual alerts.

Go with your brain. How do you remember best? Pictures, songs, rhymes, or movements can all help memory. Working with your natural abilities will help you.

TIME

WHAT IS TIME BLINDNESS?

Most brains use <u>sensory</u> information, such as light or temperature changes, to track time passing. Most brains also know roughly how many times their heart beats per minute. The brain then combines these external senses and heartbeats, which allows the brain to sense time passing.

People with ADHD find this sense of time can be weak or missing altogether. We call this time blindness. Just as visually blind people have problems sensing light, we have problems sensing time.

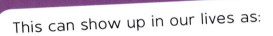

HOW LONG IS LEFT?

HOW LONG WILL THAT TAKE?

HOW LONG HAS IT BEEN SINCE...?

WHAT TIME OF DAY IS IT?

DID THAT HAPPEN BEFORE OR AFTER...?

This can show up in our lives as:

- Being really early or late, never on time
- Missing deadlines or appointments
- Having trouble making a schedule or sticking to it
- Forgetting the order of things
- Losing track of time
- Slow response times
- Having difficulty managing how fast or slowly we move
- Overestimating how much we can do in a certain time

People with ADHD either don't pick up on sensory cues or aren't able to connect them to sense time passing. Low dopamine levels also make it hard to track time, and we know that people with ADHD have lower dopamine to start with.

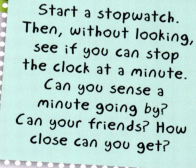

Start a stopwatch. Then, without looking, see if you can stop the clock at a minute. Can you sense a minute going by? Can your friends? How close can you get?

16

Time blindness can be very frustrating. It might sound great to forget time passing when you're playing a favorite game or reading a book, but we lose track of time even when we don't mean to — and sometimes when we REALLY don't want to. Combined with problems controlling our focus, time blindness can get in the way when we are trying to get things done. Sticking to a routine, waiting, or even doing schoolwork can be hard if you can't tell how much time is passing.

If you can't sense time passing, it can help to visualize it. Timers, especially <u>analog clocks</u> or sand timers, help us see the whole amount of time, how much has passed, and how much is left.

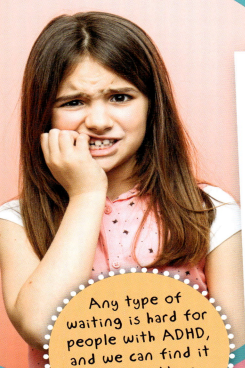

Any type of waiting is hard for people with ADHD, and we can find it very upsetting and frustrating to wait.

DAILY PLANNER

SCHEDULE	
6:00	WAITING MODE
7:00	
8:00	
9:00	
10:00	
11:00	
12:00	
1:00	
2:00	
3:00	
4:00	
5:00	
6:00	School Disco!!
7:00	
8:00	

TIME ANXIETY

Time blindness can lead to time anxiety, sometimes called "waiting mode." Not being able to sense time makes waiting very difficult. If we have something to do later, such as an exam or an appointment, we might be anxious about forgetting it or missing it. This makes us feel that we can't do anything else in case we get distracted or lose track of time. Instead, we become very focused on the event later and find it hard to do anything else beforehand. Waiting mode is tricky because we can't stop it, and it can mean an important event takes over our whole day.

TRANSITIONS
AND TASK SWITCHING

WHAT ARE TRANSITIONS?

When we switch from one thing to another, this is called a transition. Transitions come in three main types:

- **Physical Transitions** Changes to your location

- **Mental Transitions** Changes in your thoughts or **mindset**

- **Emotional Transitions** Changes in your feelings

Every transition, for example school break time, actually involves lots of small executive function tasks. We have to change location, put our books away, get a coat, and switch focus from a learning mindset to a playing one. We might also make an emotional switch from boredom to excitement. On top of all this, we have to manage time — how long do we have to get outside? How long will the break last? How much time has passed? Each of these small parts of a transition costs a little bit of energy.

A neurotypical brain can make these little transitions fit together so easily that they barely notice it. "Going out to play ball" feels like one task, so it costs a neurotypical person just a small amount of energy. But for an ADHD brain, "going out to play ball" feels like twenty tasks, so it costs twenty times as much energy. By the end of a day, we can have made hundreds of transitions and our brains can be really tired.

Transitions happen during class too — from reading to talking, from working to listening, or from thinking to discussion. How many transitions have you made today?

TASK SWITCHING AND ADHD

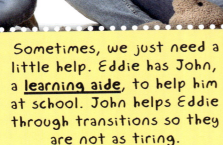

EDDIE

JOHN

Sometimes, we just need a little help. Eddie has John, a **learning aide**, to help him at school. John helps Eddie through transitions so they are not as tiring.

All of this together means switching from task to task can be challenging for a person with ADHD. Any of the small steps involved could go wrong, and this can cause anxiety around task switching. During a transition, it is easy to get distracted and end up doing something else, leaving one task unfinished and another not started. We can find it really hard to regulate our emotions during task switching too.

Taking time to rest both our bodies and our brains is extra important for people with ADHD. After school, make sure to have some quiet time to regulate and rest.

Taking extra time, especially around big transitions, is really important. People with ADHD will need more time to pull our focus out of the original activity, especially if it's exciting, interesting, or if we are hyperfocused.

Then, we need extra time to remember each step and work out how to get each one done in the right order without getting stressed or **dysregulated**. Then, it takes time to settle our focus onto a new task. Checklists, reminders, and visual aids for time can all help, as can patience and gentle guidance from people around us.

HYPERACTIVITY

A BUSY BODY

The H in ADHD stands for hyperactivity. Not everyone with ADHD will experience hyperactivity, but those of us who do know it has a big impact on our lives. Hyperactivity in the body feels like a really strong, **irresistible urge** to move — run, jump, dance, fidget, wriggle, pace, or spin. No matter how many times someone tells us to sit still, physically hyperactive people just can't. And sometimes, the more we try, the worse it feels.

"Sitting still to get my haircut is really difficult. Luckily, my barber Jonas is really patient and takes breaks so I can wriggle!" — Luke, 11 (combined type ADHD)

Sometimes, having so much energy can feel great — in sports, dancing, or running, for example. But we can't always move when we need to, and then all that energy zipping around in the body can feel very uncomfortable. Sitting still can feel so unpleasant that we can't resist the urge to move.

Movement breaks also give you more dopamine. If you're feeling fidgety, try working for 15 minutes, then dancing to one of your favorite songs. Repeat until the task is done!

A BUSY BRAIN

A person with ADHD could also have a hyperactive mind. This feels like having a brain that won't turn off, or that constantly races with ideas, thoughts, memories, and sensory information. Our minds can be so busy and noisy that we might be thinking about lots of things at once — music, conversations, questions, stories, memories, and inventions. No wonder we can't focus with all of that going on!

This can be fun and creative, or it can be totally overwhelming, depending on how we are feeling.

THINGS THAT HELP HYPERACTIVITY

A Protein-Rich Diet
Eat plenty of protein-rich foods and avoid lots of processed sugars and **carbohydrates**.

Medication
ADHD medicines can help to settle a hyperactive mind.

Exercise
20 minutes of exercise can improve your ability to focus both during and after the activity.

Mindfulness
Just 5 minutes of meditation, yoga, or listening to calming music can help.

Allies
Allies are people around us who understand us and can help us when we need it. These people understand that we really CAN'T help hyperactivity. Whether it's a teacher letting us go for an extra run around the field before a math test or a friend helping us feel calmer with a big hug, patience and understanding is very important.

Exercising outside has even greater benefits. How about a trip to the woods or a walk on the beach?

IMPULSIVITY

WHAT IS IMPULSIVITY?

An impulse is a strong feeling that you want to do something. For example, if you see a cupcake, you might feel an impulse to eat it, right? But then you find out it's actually your friend's cupcake — now you mustn't eat it, OK? You know this, but you still feel the urge to eat the cupcake, don't you? It's like a force pulling you towards it. If you give in to the feeling, you are acting on that impulse. People without ADHD are usually able to control the need to act on every impulse. Their brains give them a moment to think about it.

People without ADHD can pause and wonder whether eating the cupcake is a good idea or not. They have time to think about the consequences of giving in to all their impulses.

The ability to ignore the urge and not act on it is called impulse control. People with ADHD can have more trouble controlling our impulses than most people. When we feel an impulse to do something, it can be very intense. The need to act on it can be overwhelming, and we can't always control it at all. This means we seem to do things without thinking, such as blurting out answers in class, interrupting, or making quick decisions.

ADHD brains don't give us time to wonder if it's a good idea...

Sometimes, we can act before we even realize it.

DOPAMINE AND IMPULSIVITY

Remember dopamine — the "get things done" neurotransmitter? Well, doing impulsive things, such as shouting out a joke in class, can give us a big dopamine boost. And ADHD brains are always hungry for more dopamine, so they don't give us time to think — our brains just chase the dopamine. In an emergency, this can be really useful — we can be really fast thinkers, making quick decisions and responding immediately. In our normal, nonemergency, day-to-day life, responding so quickly to everything can cause us problems.

Adults with ADHD can be great firefighters, paramedics, or athletes. Thinking fast and responding quickly are essential parts of these jobs.

Life with us around is rarely boring — just the way we like it!

People with all types of ADHD can experience impulsivity. When we are having big feelings, such as excitement or nervousness, we can be more impulsive, and our traits will become more obvious. Impulsivity means we also really struggle with waiting and taking turns. But practice makes progress and, as you get older, you can gain some control over impulses. It's not all bad, either — people who are impulsive can be **spontaneous**, lively, and fun to be around. Our enthusiasm and energy can spread to those around us, and impulsivity and creativity go hand in hand.

MOTIVATION

DOING THE THING

Motivation is the energy that gets people to actually "do the thing" — follow the instruction, complete the task, or stay focused on that long project. People with ADHD might know we need to do the thing, but sometimes we just can't seem to get the energy to actually, you know, DO it. The harder we try to push ourselves into action, the harder it feels to actually do the thing.

It doesn't matter how much we might need to get it done, or how much people around us tell us it's important. Our brains just won't tell our bodies to do the thing.

We know that dopamine plays a big part in motivation. And we know ADHD brains can't use dopamine very well. Low-dopamine tasks (things we find boring or **repetitive**) just don't give us enough dopamine to use for motivation. To find motivation, people with ADHD need a BIG boost of dopamine. Our brains can only get excited by high-dopamine tasks. These are known as the **INCUP** motivators:

INTEREST — Exciting, complicated, or fun tasks

NOVELTY — New places, topics, methods, sensations, and experiences

CHALLENGE — Competition against others — or ourselves!

URGENCY — Rushing and racing to get something done NOW

PASSIONS — The things that matter to us as individuals, such as friendships, hobbies, interests, or **morals**

"I struggle to get motivated in school. But soccer is my passion — I never miss a training session, and I'm super focused on the pitch."
—Stanley, 10 (hyperactive type ADHD)

GET INCUP AND GO!

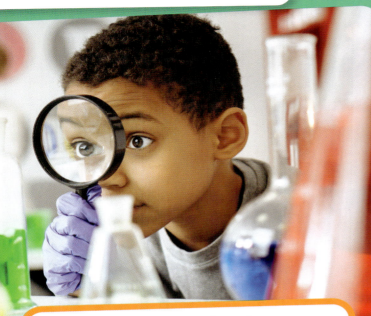

"Science is my favorite class. It's so interesting and there is always something new to find out!"
—JoJo, 11 (combined type ADHD)

In the ADHD brain, only tasks that use one or more of the INCUP motivators give us enough dopamine for us to want to "do the thing." That's why we can focus just fine on things we like, such as new interests or our passions, but struggle with boring or repetitive things that are always the same. Some things can make us so motivated that we hyperfocus and can't stop our motivation! This means we can be enthusiastic people to have around when starting an interesting new challenge or when you need something done RIGHT NOW!

FIND THE FUN!

Some tasks don't hit any of our motivators, but they still need to get done. Boring homework is still important, after all. People without ADHD can use the INCUP motivators, and they also have three more: rewards, consequences, and importance. They still get bored, but they can do the thing anyway. These three motivators just don't work in our brains. To hack our brains, we can use one of the INCUP motivators to get dopamine alongside the boring task. We could challenge ourselves to beat the clock, for example, or find a new or different place to work.

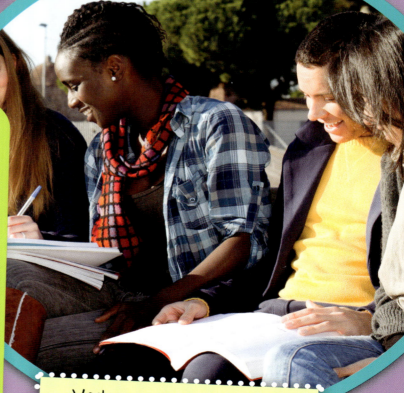

Working in a group can help us get (and stay) motivated. Friends can encourage each other, and we get dopamine from being around people we like.

EMOTIONAL REGULATION

BUSY BRAINS = BIG FEELINGS

People with ADHD can find their emotions are very "all or nothing." Even seemingly little things, such as a broken toy or someone taking our turn, can cause us to have a BIG feeling in response. Sometimes, our feelings can get so big that they are completely overwhelming. When we have a big feeling, it is very hard for us to control it. This is called emotional dysregulation. When something is causing us to have a big feeling, we focus on it and can't control our responses very well. It becomes hard to think about anything but the feeling and what we think is causing it. This is called "flooding."

One emotion can quickly flood our brains and take over. This can be a "positive" emotion such as excitement, or a "negative" emotion such as anger. When it all gets too big, it can be hard to tell the difference.

DIALS AND SWITCHES

People without ADHD usually have some control over their feelings — even big ones. This is often described like a dial, where feelings have varying levels of power. The ability to regulate emotions means people without ADHD can "dial" their feelings up or down to match the situation.

ADHD brains do not have this "dialing" ability. Our brains are more like a switch. Emotions are often either all the way on or all the way off. This means our feelings can happen very suddenly and might be much more powerful than others around us.

REJECTION SENSITIVITY

No one likes feeling rejected or like they are a failure. But for people with ADHD, this feeling can be huge, come out of nowhere, and take over our whole brain. This is so common in ADHD that it has a name: rejection sensitivity. Worrying about being rejected by others or failing in some way can take over all our feelings until we are overwhelmingly upset. We can get so worried about this that we start avoiding any potential rejection or avoid people altogether.

Is she mad at me?

Will anyone come to my party?

Did I say that right?

REGULATING EMOTIONS

It can take a little extra time to regulate such big emotions. While it is difficult, especially for children with ADHD, emotional regulation skills can be learned.

- Just taking a deep breath is a good start.

- Naming your feelings can help you understand them.

- Use your favorite way to express your feelings — write, draw, dance, or exercise your feelings out.

- Mindfulness can help in a stressful moment.

- Practice makes progress — these skills will come with time, so have patience (if you can!).

FAMOUS

PEOPLE WITH ADHD

SIMONE BILES

Simone Biles is an American gymnast — and not just any gymnast. Simone's fans call her the GOAT, meaning the "greatest of all time," and for a good reason. Simone has broken many world records and won more medals than any gymnast ever. She has also competed in the Olympics many times throughout her incredible career.

SIMONE FIRST TRIED GYMNASTICS AT AGE SIX.

DAV PILKEY

Just like his characters, Dav drew his cartoons despite his teachers saying they would never amount to anything... but they were wrong!

As a young child, Dav Pilkey had trouble concentrating and sitting still. Dav has both ADHD and dyslexia, and he often found himself sent out of class for talking... where he wrote and drew a comic book in the hall to pass the time. That comic book went on to become the worldwide hit series Captain Underpants! His parents supported him and now, over twenty years later, this hyperfocus is still going! Dav calls ADHD "Attention Deficit Hyperactivity Delightfulness" and says it is the reason his stories are not boring.

CHANNING TATUM

Channing Tatum is an American actor, model, and dancer. After struggling in school, he moved to New York and found he learned best from other people, instead of sitting in a classroom. He found the arts and danced his way to success with movies including *Step Up* and *G.I. Joe*. Despite struggling with reading and focus, dance and performance gave him a channel for his energy and creativity. He is now a famous celebrity and makes his own movies.

BEX TAYLOR-KLAUS

Bex Taylor-Klaus is an American actor with ADHD. Bex really struggled in school, eventually getting kicked out of their mainstream school. But they went on and found acting success young, when they landed a role in a TV show, and their career hasn't stopped since. Bex also supports others with ADHD and helps people understand what life with ADHD is really like.

QUESTIONS

DO I HAVE ADHD?

If you didn't think you had ADHD before reading this book, but you recognize some of the things we talked about, you might be wondering whether you are neurodivergent yourself. If that's you, talk to a trusted adult who can help you find out. If you are struggling or feel like you need help, it's OK to ask for it. You don't have to cope alone, and people can help you feel better about the world.

Usually, you will start with your doctor, and then see a specialist doctor to diagnose you. You would then do an assessment with your grown-ups, who will talk to the doctor. The doctor will ask you some questions and give you some activities to do. This will help them work out what's going on.

Recognizing a few traits doesn't mean you have ADHD. But if you recognized a lot of things, you might be wondering... could this diagnosis be right for me?

An ADHD diagnosis can help you understand yourself better.

Finding out you have ADHD can be a surprise, and for many people it is a relief. Often, it is better to know yourself and understand your brain, so you can change and shape your life to suit you and your needs.

If you do have ADHD, hopefully this book has helped you learn a little more about yourself. ADHD research is changing all the time, so there are always new things to learn about our big, beautiful brains!

GLOSSARY

ALLY — a person who is not part of a certain community but supports and stands up for members of the community

ANALOG CLOCKS — clocks with numbers and moving hands

CARBOHYDRATES — foods that give us energy and contain sugar and starch

CHEMICALS — substances that cannot be broken down without being changed into something else

DIAGNOSED — when a condition is recognized by a doctor

DISABILITY — a condition or difference of the body or mind that makes some activities more difficult or impossible to do

DYSREGULATED — feeling big feelings that are hard to understand and control

EMPATHY — understanding how other people feel

HIGH PROTEIN MEALS — meals that contain a lot of a nutrient called protein

IRRESISTIBLE URGE — a strong, unavoidable desire or need to do something

LEARNING AIDE — a person who works to help someone learn, such as by helping them with challenges at school

MINDFULNESS — being aware of yourself, your mind, and your feelings

MINDSET — a state of mind

MOLECULE — the smallest piece of something

MORALS — ideas of right and wrong

REGULATE — to control

REPETITIVE — something that happens over and over again

SENSORY — relating to the senses, such as sight and smell

SPONTANEOUS — something unplanned and unexpected

STIMMING — "self-stimulatory behavior," or doing repeated movements to stimulate your own senses

VITAMINS AND MINERALS — substances that your body uses to work properly and stay healthy

INDEX